BETRAYED

"WHEN CHOICES COLLIDE WITH CONSEQUENCES"

PRUDANCE VANESSA NDHLOVU

To my beloved parents,
Fungai Ndhlovu and Sydney Ndhlovu,
for your unwavering love, guidance, and sacrifices that
have shaped the person I am today.

To my dear sisters,
Privilege Thelma Ndhlovu and Pria Buhlebenkosi
Ndhlovu,
for being my pillars of support, my constant cheerleaders,
and my source of strength.

This book is for you—thank you for believing in me and
inspiring me every day.

Contents

Foreword

The journey of Aisha in Betrayed is one that mirrors the struggles of many young women who navigate love, betrayal, and redemption. This story invites readers to explore the depths of human emotion, the consequences of choices, and the strength it takes to rebuild one's life. Prudance Vanessa Ndhlovu masterfully weaves a tale that is both heartbreaking and hopeful, offering insights into relationships, family bonds, and the transformative power of forgiveness. As you turn these pages, you'll find not just a story, but a reflection of resilience and the enduring quest for self-discovery.

PREFACE

The inspiration for Betrayed arose from a desire to address the challenges many young people face when they are caught between societal expectations and their personal struggles. Through Aisha's journey, I sought to explore themes of identity, the weight of past mistakes, and the courage required to confront one's demons. This story is deeply personal, yet universal in its resonance, touching on issues that many of us may face at some point in our lives. It is my hope that readers find a piece of themselves in Aisha's journey and come away with a renewed sense of compassion for themselves and others.

Acknowledgements

First and foremost, I give thanks to God for the strength, inspiration, and grace that guided me through the writing of this book. Without His presence in my life, this story would not have been possible.

To my family, your love and support mean the world to me. You've stood by me through every challenge, celebrated every milestone, and believed in my dreams even when they seemed far away. I am eternally grateful.

To my friends, thank you for your encouragement and for being my sounding boards. Your feedback, enthusiasm, and patience have been invaluable throughout this journey.

To my readers, thank you for trusting me with your time and emotions. Your willingness to journey through Aisha's story means more than words can express.

Finally, to everyone who has faced struggles similar to those in Betrayed, know that you are not alone. May this book serve as a reminder that redemption, hope, and love are always within reach.

With gratitude,
Prudance Vanessa Ndhlovu

PROLOGUE

The choices we make define the paths we tread. For Aisha, the path to heartbreak began with a single decision: to let her guard down in the pursuit of love. Beneath the laughter and smiles of university life, a storm was brewing—one that would strip her of innocence, test her faith, and push her to the very edge of despair. This is not just a story of loss, but one of redemption and finding hope in the unlikeliest of places. Before the betrayal, there was trust. Before the despair, there was love. And at the heart of it all lies a truth Aisha must confront.

I

A New Beginning

I sat in the quiet corner of our living room, my hands trembling as I held the letter. The thick, cream-colored envelope felt heavy, almost like it was carrying the weight of my entire future. I had been waiting for this moment for weeks—hoping, praying, that I had done enough. I'd worked tirelessly, putting in the late nights, the sacrifices, and the effort to prove to myself—and everyone else—that I was capable of more. This was my chance to show that I could achieve something great.

As I slowly opened the envelope, I felt my heart race. The anticipation gripped me. I scanned the words quickly, my eyes moving over the sentences, each one a puzzle piece falling into place. Then, finally, the truth hit me—I had passed. Not just passed—I'd excelled. I let out a breath I didn't even realize I was holding, and a rush of pride and relief swept over me. All the hard work, all the moments I doubted myself, had led to this. I had done it.

I could feel my parents' presence in the doorway before I even looked up. My mom was the first to pull me into her arms, her soft smile making my chest tighten with emotion.

"I'm so proud of you, Aisha," she whispered, her voice full of love and pride.

And then my dad, always the quiet one, gave me a nod of approval. "You did it, my daughter," he said, his voice steady but thick with emotion. "Remember, this is just the beginning. Keep God at the center of your life, and you will go far. Whatever comes next, don't ever forget where your strength comes from."

I nodded, the weight of his words settling deep in my heart. I'd always known that their faith was the foundation of everything they did. It had guided them through life, and they had instilled it in me since I was young. The reminder to keep God close, especially when life became challenging, was something I promised to carry with me into this new chapter of my life.

With high school behind me, the next step was university. It felt like the beginning of something huge, a dream I had always held close to my heart. I was excited, yes, but there was also an undeniable pressure. University wouldn't be easy, and I knew the road ahead would be full of challenges. But this was what I had worked for.

And then there was Adin's. My older brother, always protective of me, had watched me work so hard to get to this point. He saw how much effort I had put into my studies, and as a way to support me, he surprised me with something I never expected.

A car.

The shiny new vehicle gleamed under the sun as I stood there, staring at it in disbelief. I couldn't quite process it at first. A car? For me? This wasn't something I had imagined, not at my age. The keys rested in my palm like a symbol of independence, of possibility.

"This is for you, Aisha," Adin's said with a grin, his eyes filled with pride. "To help you get to and from university. I know you'll need it."

I couldn't find the words. "Thank you," I whispered, my voice catching in my throat as I hugged him tightly. He had always been there for me, through thick and thin, and this gesture only reminded me how lucky I was to have him in my life.

In the days that followed, I settled into my new routine. The car gave me a sense of freedom I hadn't felt before. No more relying on others to get to school—I could drive myself, which felt like such a small thing, but also such a big deal. It was a step toward independence, and for the first time, I truly felt like I was in control of my own future.

It was during one of these drives that I met Samantha. It had been a busy day at university, and I had just parked my car when I saw a girl standing by the entrance, looking a bit lost. She had that look in her eyes—the kind that said, "I'm trying to figure things out, but I'm not quite there yet."

I walked over to her with a smile. "Hey, you alright?"

Her face lit up with relief, and I could almost feel her tension melt away. "Yeah, just trying to figure out where my next class is," she said, laughing nervously. "I'm new here, and everything feels a bit overwhelming."

"I know exactly how you feel," I said, nodding in understanding. "I'm new too. I'm Aisha, by the way. Let me know if you need help finding anything."

From that moment on, we just clicked.

II

A Tangled Web

Samantha, my self-proclaimed best friend, was everything my mother had warned me about. She was tall and striking in her army green jumpsuit, exuding an air of confidence that bordered on arrogance. Samantha had a magnetic energy, drawing people into her orbit effortlessly. Her loud laughter often echoed through the university hallways, making her the center of attention wherever she went.

Despite our differences, I was eager to connect with her. Samantha represented a world of excitement and freedom that I had never experienced. Blinded by my yearning for companionship, I accepted her friendship without question.

Samantha's charm was intoxicating. She had a way of making you feel like the most important person in the room, yet her influence was far from positive. It wasn't long before I began to notice her manipulative tendencies. She would encourage me to skip classes, whispering, "Aisha, live a little! Life is too short to be spent buried in books." Her words felt liberating in the moment, but they carried consequences I wasn't prepared for.

One afternoon, as we sat under the sprawling shade of a jacaranda tree, Samantha's mischievous grin appeared. "I have something for you," she said, pulling a small, ornate bottle from her bag. It was a perfume she claimed was from an exclusive brand. "A gift for my favorite friend," she declared, but the undertone of manipulation in her voice didn't escape me.

Despite my reservations, I found myself drawn deeper into Samantha's world. Her stories of late-night adventures, secret parties, and forbidden relationships were tantalizing. She spoke of her cousin Kate, a medical student and fellow church member, as the "saint" of the family, a stark contrast to her own rebellious nature. Samantha often mocked Kate's righteousness, saying, "She's a bore who lives by the rules. Who needs that?"

Samantha's world collided with mine in unexpected ways. During one of our lectures, my gaze kept drifting to the boy with the captivating eyes—Ryan. His name lingered in the air, a melody both inviting and dangerous. Samantha, ever the opportunist, noticed my interest and made it her mission to play matchmaker.

"Ryan? Oh, I know him," Samantha said with a smirk. "He's trouble, but I think you could handle him." Her words were laced with mischief, as though she relished the idea of setting me up for an adventure I wasn't ready for.

The arrival of a young, distinguished lecturer momentarily stole my attention. He exuded authority, his sharp gaze scanning the room as he began his lecture. This was university life, a stark departure from the sheltered existence I had known. The thrill of this new chapter filled me with a mix of excitement and trepidation.

As the days turned into weeks, Samantha's influence grew. She persuaded me to attend a party at her apartment, a world alien to my values. "It's just a small gathering," she said, her voice dripping with enthusiasm. Reluctantly, I agreed, not wanting to disappoint her. That night, as the music blared and laughter filled the air, I felt like an imposter. The carefree revelry around me was exhilarating, yet it clashed with the principles my family had instilled in me.

Samantha, ever the life of the party, introduced me to Ryan, who seemed to have been waiting for this moment. His charming demeanor and easy smile made my heart race. Samantha watched our interaction with a knowing look, her satisfaction evident. She had orchestrated this meeting, pulling the strings like a master puppeteer.

As I navigated this new chapter of my life, I began to see the cracks in Samantha's facade. Her confidence masked insecurities she rarely acknowledged. Despite her outward bravado, there were moments when her vulnerability peeked through—a wistful glance, a quiet sigh. Yet, she never allowed herself to dwell on these feelings, choosing instead to lose herself in the chaos she created.

In Samantha, I found both a friend and a cautionary tale. She embodied the allure of freedom but also the dangers of straying too far from one's path. As our friendship deepened, I couldn't shake the feeling that I was teetering on the edge of something profound and irreversible. The tangled web Samantha wove around me was both thrilling and suffocating, a testament to the complexity of her character and the choices I faced.

III

The Dark Side of Friendship

Samantha, once my confidante, had become a catalyst for my downfall. It was her relentless insistence that I attend her parties, a world alien to my values, that had first drawn me away from God's path. And it was her manipulative nature that had led me to Ryan, a man who would become the architect of my destruction.

One afternoon, as I navigated the university campus, Samantha's voice cut through the noise. "Aisha, you have to come to my party tonight!" She pleaded, her eyes wide with excitement. I hesitated, the familiar guilt gnawing at me. I knew it was wrong, yet the allure of acceptance was too strong. Reluctantly, I agreed, a decision I would soon regret.

That night, I found myself lost in a sea of unfamiliar faces, the music pounding in my ears. Alcohol flowed freely, and I found myself drawn into the intoxicating rhythm. My inhibitions faded, replaced by a reckless abandon. It was a world I didn't belong in, a world that clashed with the principles I had been taught.

As the night wore on, I felt a growing sense of unease. Something was amiss. A premonition, perhaps. But I ignored it, lost in the moment. It wasn't until I found myself alone with Ryan that the truth began to unravel. He confessed his love for me, his words laced with a sincerity that seemed almost genuine. My heart raced, a whirlwind of emotions swirling within me. I knew I should resist, but the desire for love, for acceptance, blinded me.

In that moment, I made the biggest mistake of my life. I said yes.

IV

The Downward Spiral

The relationship with Ryan was a whirlwind, a consuming passion that overshadowed everything else in my life. I neglected my studies, my faith, and even my family. My mother's warnings faded into a distant memory, replaced by the intoxicating thrill of being in love.

Ryan showered me with affection, with gifts, with promises of a future together. But beneath the surface, a darkness lurked. He was manipulative, controlling, and increasingly possessive. I was trapped in a web of his own creation, unable to break free.

One evening, as I sat with Ryan in a secluded park, he revealed his deepest secret. His mother was sick, suffering from a terminal illness. He needed money for her treatment, a staggering amount that I knew my family couldn't afford. Desperate, I made a decision that would haunt me forever.

I stole from my father. The thought of betraying his trust filled me with dread, but my love for Ryan blinded me to the consequences. I forged documents, withdrew the money, and handed it over to Ryan. In that moment, I crossed a line I never thought I would.

The Betrayal Revealed

The weight of my actions was unbearable. I had betrayed my family, my values, and my own conscience. The guilt was a constant companion, a heavy burden that I carried with me everywhere. Yet, I clung to the hope that Ryan would use the money as he had promised.

Days turned into weeks, and still, there was no news about Ryan's mother. My anxiety grew, a gnawing suspicion taking hold. I confronted Ryan, demanding answers. His evasive behavior only fueled my suspicions. Something was terribly wrong.

One evening, as I sat alone in my room, lost in thought, I heard a commotion downstairs. My mother burst into my room, her face pale and her eyes filled with tears. She told me that Ryan had been arrested for drug smuggling. The stolen money, the lies, everything was a carefully orchestrated plan. My heart shattered into a million pieces.

I had been betrayed, not just by Ryan, but by my own naivety and blind trust. The reality of my actions hit me like a ton of bricks. I had not only betrayed my family but also my faith.

VI
Consequences of Betrayal

The morning after my mother's tearful revelation of Ryan's arrest, I sat motionless in the living room, my mind a whirlwind of emotions. I had given him everything—my trust, my heart, and even the money I stole from my family. And now, it was all gone, swept away in a tide of deceit.

The shame of my actions weighed heavily on me. I couldn't look my parents in the eye. My father's silence was louder than any words of condemnation, and my mother's prayers echoed through the house, each one a plea for mercy and redemption.

I wanted to hide from the world, but the world had other plans for me. A knock at the door jolted me from my thoughts. My heart raced as I saw two uniformed officers standing on the porch.

"Miss Aisha, we need you to come with us for questioning," one of them said, his voice firm yet not unkind.

My knees buckled beneath me. "Questioning? About what?" I asked, though I already knew the answer.

They explained that Ryan had implicated me during his interrogation. According to him, I was not just an unwitting accomplice but an active participant in his schemes. My stomach churned with anger and disbelief. How could he do this to me?

At the police station, the interrogation room felt cold and oppressive. The officer across from me laid out the evidence: the forged documents, the stolen money, and my connection to Ryan. Every piece of proof felt like a dagger to my chest.

"I didn't know," I whispered, tears streaming down my face. "I thought he needed the money for his mother's treatment."

The officer's expression softened slightly, but the law wasn't swayed by my naivety. "You may not have known the full extent of his actions, but you were complicit in stealing the money. That makes you an accessory."

As I sat in the holding cell, trembling and confused, an unfamiliar face appeared—a tall man with a cold smile who introduced himself as one of Ryan's "associates." His voice was calm, but his words sent a chill down my spine.

"You owe us, Aisha," he said flatly. "Ryan's mess doesn't end with his arrest. We need you to deliver something for us. Do this, and we'll make sure your name isn't dragged any further into this."

I stared at him, horrified. "I don't want any part of this," I stammered.

"You don't have a choice," he said, leaning closer. "Unless you want us to make sure the cops dig deeper into what you and Ryan were up to."

Desperation clouded my judgment. Terrified of what else could come to light—and clinging to a naïve hope that this would clear my name—I agreed. The task was simple: retrieve a package from a storage unit and deliver it to an address they would provide.

The moment I stepped into the storage unit, my stomach turned. Inside the package were bags of drugs—far more than I had imagined. Panic surged through me. I shouldn't have come, shouldn't have agreed. But it was too late. As I left, clutching the package, I was intercepted by police officers who had been tipped off about the delivery.

The confrontation turned chaotic. I tried to explain that I was coerced, that I didn't know what I was carrying. But my panic only made me look guilty. In the scuffle that followed, one of the officers fell, hitting his head on the pavement. He was rushed to the hospital but didn't survive the night.

When the charges were read to me, I felt the weight of the world collapse on my shoulders. Fraud, theft, drug trafficking, and involuntary manslaughter. My lawyer tried to argue that I had been manipulated and that I wasn't responsible for the officer's death, but the evidence painted a damning picture.

The trial was swift, and the verdict was harsher than I could have imagined. Twenty-five years. My mother's sobs echoed through the courtroom as the sentence was read. My father's face was a mask of pain and disappointment. I couldn't even bring myself to look at Adin.

The day I was taken to jail was the darkest of my life. My mother's cries followed me as I walked away in handcuffs, and my father didn't say a word.

VII
Hope

As I sat in the prison, my mind raced with thoughts of the past. The betrayal, the lies, the consequences of my actions. But one thought lingered, a heavy weight on my conscience. My pregnancy. I had been pregnant, a fact I had buried deep within myself, a secret I had kept hidden even from myself.

The thought of my unborn child filled me with a mix of guilt and sorrow. I had brought this child into the world, only to abandon it. The pain of that realization was almost unbearable.

With newfound determination, I resolved to make amends. I wrote a letter to the adoption agency, expressing my desire to give my child a chance at a better life. I knew it was a selfless act, but it was also a way to atone for my past mistakes.

The days turned into weeks, and I began to feel the physical changes of pregnancy. My body ached, and my appetite soared. Yet, I kept my condition a secret, fearing the judgment and rejection that would surely follow.

The days in prison blurred into weeks, and my secret became harder to conceal. My growing belly was a constant reminder of the life within me, a fragile hope I didn't know I deserved. I avoided questions, wore loose clothing, and kept to myself, but the other inmates began to notice. Whispers filled the air—speculation, judgment, and curiosity.

One night, as I lay on the hard mattress in my cell, a kind-hearted inmate named Grace approached me. She was older, with gray streaks in her braided hair and a wisdom in her eyes that spoke of her own battles.

"You can't hide it forever, Aisha," she said gently, sitting on the edge of my bed. "You're going to be a mother, and that's nothing to be ashamed of."

Her words cut through my fear, but they also left me conflicted. What kind of mother could I be from behind these bars? How could I bring a child into a world where I couldn't even provide for myself?

The weeks passed, and the time came when my secret could no longer remain hidden. The prison staff noticed my condition during a routine medical check, and soon, everyone knew. My family was informed, and I braced myself for their reaction.

When my parents visited, their faces were a mix of heartbreak and concern. My mother reached for my hand through the glass divider. "Aisha, why didn't you tell us? We could have helped you," she said, tears streaming down her face.

But I couldn't meet her gaze. "I didn't want you to bear the shame, Mama," I whispered. "This is my burden to carry."

My father sat silently, his hands clasped tightly, his expression unreadable. Finally, he spoke. "Let us take the child, Aisha. Your mother and I will raise them until you come home."

Their offer was kind, selfless even, but I couldn't accept it. The weight of societal judgment on my family was too much to bear. I had already stained their reputation with my actions. Bringing a child into their lives under such circumstances would only add to their pain.

"I can't," I said, my voice trembling. "I've already made up my mind. The baby will be placed for adoption. It's the only way to give them a chance at a better life."

My mother sobbed, and my father's face hardened with resignation. They didn't agree with my decision, but they respected it.

As the months passed, I prepared for the inevitable. I worked with a social worker from the adoption agency, carefully selecting a family who would give my child the love and stability I couldn't provide. They were a kind couple who had longed for a child of their own—a doctor and a teacher, living in a quiet suburb.

The day of my labor arrived unexpectedly, marked by sharp pains that left me gasping in my cell. The prison staff rushed me to the infirmary, and hours later, I gave birth to a beautiful baby girl. Tears streamed down my face as I held her for the first time, her tiny fingers wrapping around mine.

"I'll call you Hope," I whispered. "Because you're the light in my darkest hour."

The next few days were bittersweet. I cherished every moment with Hope, memorizing her face, her scent, the way her tiny lips curved into the faintest smile. But I knew our time together was fleeting.

The day I handed her over to the adoption agency was the hardest of my life. I kissed her forehead one last time, whispering a prayer for her happiness. "I'm so sorry," I said, my voice breaking. "I love you more than anything, and that's why I have to let you go."

As the social worker walked away with Hope in her arms, I felt a piece of my heart leave with her. Back in my cell, the emptiness was overwhelming, but I clung to the belief that I had made the right choice—for her, if not for me.

In the weeks that followed, I received a letter from the adoptive parents, thanking me for entrusting them with such a precious gift. They promised to give Hope a life filled with love and opportunity, and while it didn't erase the ache in my heart, it gave me a sense of peace.

Though I had lost so much, I found a sliver of redemption in my sacrifice. Hope was my second chance, even if I couldn't be a part of her life. And as I marked the days until my release, I held onto the dream that one day, she would know how deeply she was loved.

VIII

A Second Chance

Years passed, and I served my sentence. The prison walls had become a familiar part of my existence, a constant reminder of the mistakes I had made. Yet, I clung to hope, a tiny flame that refused to be extinguished.

Upon my release, I returned to a world that felt both familiar and foreign. My family had distanced themselves, their fear of judgment outweighing their love for me. I was alone, but I was determined to rebuild my life.

I found work, a small apartment, and a sense of normalcy. The memory of Hope haunted me, a constant reminder of the child I had given up. I wondered about her, about her life, her happiness.

One day, while browsing through old newspapers, I stumbled upon a story about a young woman who had won a prestigious award for her work in environmental conservation. Her name was Hope. A wave of emotion washed over me as I read the article. Could it be?

Driven by a mix of curiosity and hope, I reached out to the organization mentioned in the article. To my astonishment, they confirmed that Hope was my daughter.

The news was overwhelming. I felt a mix of joy, relief, and a pang of guilt. I had given her up, yet she had thrived. I longed to meet her, to know her, to make amends.

With trembling hands, I wrote a letter, pouring out my heart and soul. Weeks later, I received a reply. Hope agreed to meet me.

Our reunion was a bittersweet moment. We talked for hours, sharing our stories, our dreams, our fears. I learned about the incredible woman Hope had become, a testament to her resilience and spirit.

As we parted ways, I knew that my journey was far from over. The past would always be a part of me, but it would no longer define me. I had found redemption, not only for myself but also for my daughter. And in that, I found peace.

IX

The Wedding Revelation

I stood outside the grand church, my fingers nervously adjusting the scarf around my neck. The building loomed before me, majestic and imposing, but inside, I knew a storm was brewing—one that I had no right to be a part of. For hours, I had debated whether or not to come. Hope had made it clear that she didn't want me there. "It's a private day," she had said, her voice polite but distant, the way it always was when she set boundaries.

I didn't blame her. We had only reconnected a few months ago, and though she had agreed to meet her biological mother, I knew that she was still keeping me at arm's length, unwilling to let me fully into her life. I had expected this. But when Mrs. Daniels, Hope's adoptive mother, casually mentioned the wedding date and venue in one of our rare conversations, something inside me stirred. It wasn't just curiosity—it was a longing, a desire to see Hope happy, even if it meant watching from a distance.

So here I was.

I wasn't here to cause trouble, I told myself. I just wanted to see my daughter on her special day. Even if I had to do it from the shadows.

As I slipped into the back of the church just as the ceremony began, I tried to keep to myself, to stay out of sight. My heart raced, each footstep feeling like a heavy echo in the silence. I avoided eye contact with the guests, keeping my gaze fixed on the floor as I found a seat in the back pew.

And then she walked down the aisle.

Hope.

She was stunning, radiating an ethereal beauty that made my chest tighten. Her smile was radiant, like a beacon, lighting up the entire room. I felt a swell of pride in my chest, followed by a pang of joy—a joy I hadn't allowed myself to feel in so long. This was my daughter, the one I had prayed for, the one I had given up for a better life. Seeing her here, in this moment, it was everything I had ever wanted for her.

But as the groom turned to face her, something stopped me cold.

His face.

It was familiar. Hauntingly familiar.

I could feel my heart drop into my stomach. Time had aged him, but there was no mistaking it. Ryan. The man who had shattered my life. The man who had betrayed me. And now, he was standing there, about to marry my daughter.

A wave of nausea hit me. I gripped the back of the pew in front of me, my legs trembling beneath me. I wanted to run, to flee from the church and pretend that I hadn't seen any of this. But I couldn't. Not when I knew the truth.

The ceremony continued, the vows drawing nearer, but I could hardly hear them over the rush of blood in my ears. I was frozen, unable to look away from Ryan.

The officiant's voice broke through my thoughts. "Ryan, please state your full name."

"Ryan Matthew Carter," he said confidently, the words slicing through me like a blade.

Before I realized it, a whisper slipped from my lips. "No."

It was barely audible, but it was enough. The room fell silent. Eyes turned to me, and I felt the heat of their gaze like an unbearable weight.

I couldn't stop myself.

"This can't happen!" My voice was trembling now, rising with desperation.

Hope froze at the altar, her face a mix of shock and horror. She didn't understand. She couldn't.

"What are you doing here?" she demanded, her voice sharp with anger.

I ignored her, my gaze locked on Ryan, my heart pounding in my chest. "Do you even know who she is?" I couldn't stop myself from asking. My voice was shaking now, raw with emotion.

Ryan's confusion was apparent as he looked between Hope and me. "Who is this?" he asked, his brow furrowed.

"I'm Aisha," I said, my voice breaking with the weight of it. "The woman you left behind. The woman you betrayed. And she—" I pointed toward Hope, my hand trembling, "is your daughter."

Gasps filled the room. Hope staggered backward, her bouquet slipping from her hands.

"No," she whispered, shaking her head as if she could deny the truth.

Ryan's face turned pale. "What is she talking about?" he asked, turning to Hope, his voice full of panic.

Hope turned to me, her eyes blazing with anger and disbelief. "You're lying," she spat, her voice low and furious. "This is just another one of your attempts to ruin my life."

"I'm not lying," I said, stepping closer, my breath shaky. "Check the adoption records. You'll see. It's all there."

Hope's knees buckled, and she grabbed the altar rail for support. Her breath came in ragged gasps, tears streaming down her face as she turned to Ryan, searching his eyes for answers.

"You knew, didn't you?" she whispered, her voice trembling. "You knew there was something off about us, about all of this."

Ryan shook his head, his voice frantic. "I didn't know! I swear, I had no idea."

Hope's hands instinctively went to her stomach, her face pale as realization hit her. "I'm pregnant," she whispered, barely audible. "I'm pregnant with your child. My half-sibling."

The room erupted into chaos. The air was thick with whispers, and people began standing up, some leaving, others staring in stunned silence.

Ryan turned away, his face frozen in shock and horror. Hope collapsed onto a nearby chair, sobbing uncontrollably.

I wanted to go to her, to comfort her, but she held up a hand, stopping me. "Don't," she said, her voice full of venom. "You've done enough."

"I didn't know," I whispered, the words coming out in a broken breath. "If I had, I would have told you. I only came here to see you happy, not to ruin your day."

"Well, congratulations," Hope snapped, her voice dripping with bitterness. "You've succeeded."

I stood frozen, my heart breaking as I watched my daughter crumble. I had prayed for this moment—for a chance to show her I wasn't the monster she thought I was. But now, it felt like all those prayers had been in vain.

As the guests began filing out, Mrs. Daniels approached me, her face filled with pity. "You should go," she said gently. "She needs time."

I nodded, my tears falling freely now. I turned and walked out of the church, my head bowed. I had come hoping to witness a moment of love, but I was leaving with nothing but chaos in my wake.

X

The Weight of Regret

The days that followed the wedding were a blur. My apartment, once a place of quiet refuge, now felt like a prison. I couldn't escape the image of Hope's face, streaked with tears, the pain etched in her eyes like a permanent scar. It haunted me. Every time I closed my eyes, I saw her—standing there at the altar, her world shattered by a truth I had hoped would never be revealed.

Guilt gnawed at me, relentless and unforgiving. I had tried to protect her, to shield her from the ugly parts of my past. But now, it felt like I had done nothing but expose her to more hurt. Each memory of her innocence, of the girl I had hoped would grow up free from the weight of my mistakes, seemed to mock me. I had failed her.

I couldn't escape the truth. My decisions had cost me more than I had ever anticipated. The love I had wanted to give her, the life I had dreamed for her, felt out of reach. She was no longer the little girl I had left behind. She was a woman, caught in the mess I had made, and I wasn't sure if I could ever fix it.

I spent my days in solitude, my thoughts drowning in regret. The quiet only amplified the turmoil within me. What kind of future could I offer her now? Was there any hope of redemption, or had I irreparably damaged everything?

I thought of Hope again—of her grief, compounded now by her pregnancy. It should have been a joyous time, the beginning of new life, but instead, it had become a reminder of everything she wished she could undo. The excitement she had once felt about the child growing inside her had been replaced with fear. Fear of the unknown, fear of what kind of future she could offer her baby when everything in her life felt so broken.

Hope didn't want to face anyone. She withdrew further into herself, retreating into the quiet of her room, where she could hide from the concern of her adoptive family. They didn't know everything. They didn't understand what had happened between us, between me and Ryan. I couldn't bring myself to tell them. How could I explain everything? How could I ask for their forgiveness when I didn't know how to forgive myself?

The guilt was suffocating, and I wasn't sure where to turn. I knew I had hurt Hope, but Ryan, too, was drowning in his own regret. He had no idea about the child he had fathered until that moment, and now, he couldn't look at himself without feeling disgusted by the path he had taken. His relationship with Hope, his involvement in her pain—it was too much for him to bear. But it was the past with me that weighed the heaviest on his soul.

I hadn't expected him to reach out to me, but he did. He wanted to mend something. Anything. He wanted to fix the mess we had made. But how could he? How could he fix something so utterly broken? Every time he called, I couldn't bring myself to answer. Our conversations, when they did happen, were cold, distant. Like two strangers trying to remember who they once were.

Ryan was paralyzed by guilt, just as I was. What could he say to Hope? To me? How could he explain the weight of his actions when everything felt so beyond repair? He wanted to make amends, but I could see the fear in his eyes. The fear that it was too late, that the damage was irreversible.

And so we all stood at a crossroads—Hope, Ryan, and I—uncertain of what came next. The choices we had made had brought us here, but we couldn't see the road ahead. Would we find a way to rebuild the pieces of what we had destroyed? Or would we continue to be trapped in the suffocating grip of our regrets, forever haunted by the lives we had torn apart?

Each of us had our own struggles, our own burdens to bear. But in the end, we were all asking the same question: is there a way back from here?

XI

The Weight of Words

I knew I couldn't hide from this forever. The guilt was suffocating, but what hurt more was the silence between me and Hope. The silence I had created. I had to speak to her—had to explain myself, even if it meant facing the consequences of everything I had done. I had wronged her in ways I couldn't even begin to describe, and the longer I waited, the heavier that burden grew.

It wasn't easy, standing in front of Hope. There was so much between us now, so many unsaid words, so many unhealed wounds. She had every right to be angry, to hate me. But I had to try, for her sake and for mine.

When I knocked on the door, I could hear her moving inside, the soft shuffle of footsteps, the hesitant pause before she opened it. Hope's eyes met mine, and I saw the storm in them—the hurt, the confusion, the betrayal. She didn't say anything at first. She didn't need to. The walls were up, as they had been since the wedding, and I wasn't sure if I could tear them down.

"I don't want to hear any more excuses, Aisha," she finally said, her voice cold, distant. "You've done enough."

Her words stung, but I couldn't back down. Not now. "I don't have any excuses," I said softly, stepping into the room. "I just... I just need you to understand why I did what I did. I need you to understand that it wasn't because I didn't love you. It wasn't because I didn't want you. It was because I thought I was doing what was best for you."

Hope's arms crossed tightly over her chest, a defense mechanism I had seen all too often. She was protecting herself, and I couldn't blame her. "Best for me?" she repeated bitterly. "You left me. You abandoned me without any explanation. You made me feel like I wasn't worth fighting for."

"I know," I whispered, the weight of her words sinking into my bones. "I'm sorry, Hope. I'm so sorry. I wasn't strong enough. I didn't know how to be the mother you deserved. I thought... I thought if I let go, you'd have a better life. I thought it would be easier for you."

Hope's face twisted with disbelief. "Easier for me? How? By making me wonder every day why you didn't want me? By leaving me with strangers and pretending like you didn't exist? Do you have any idea what that did to me?"

Her words were a slap to my face, but they were the truth. She had every right to be angry. "I wasn't trying to hurt you," I said, my voice cracking. "I thought I was saving you from a life that would have been filled with too many complications, too much pain. I thought you deserved more than I could give you, Hope. And I—" I paused, trying to steady my breath, "I was wrong."

There was a long silence between us. Hope's eyes softened for a moment, but I could tell she was still torn.

She wasn't ready to forgive me, but maybe, just maybe, she was starting to understand.

"I don't know if I can forgive you, Aisha," she said quietly, her voice filled with vulnerability I hadn't expected. "But I'm listening. For the first time, I'm actually listening."

And that was all I needed. I had to make things right, even if it meant taking it slow, even if it meant facing the consequences of my mistakes one painful step at a time.

Ryan reached out to Hope the next day. I didn't know what to expect from him—what he wanted, what he hoped to achieve—but I knew that whatever it was, he couldn't keep running from the truth anymore. Hope's pregnancy, our shared past, it had all come crashing down on him, just like it had for me.

"I need to talk to you, Hope," Ryan's voice came through her phone, shaky and uncertain. "Please, just... let me explain."

Hope didn't respond right away, and I could see her hesitation. I could feel it in the air, heavy between us. But she didn't hang up, didn't shut him out completely. She let him speak, which I took as a good sign.

"I messed up," Ryan continued, his voice thick with regret. "I should have been there. I should have been honest with you, with myself. And now I don't know how to make up for it. But I want to be part of this, part of your life, and part of our child's life. I can't change the past, but I want to try to make it right."

Hope was silent for a long time. I could see her wrestling with her emotions, torn between the anger that had been bubbling inside her and the need for stability for the child she carried. She wanted to forgive him, I could tell, but the wounds were still fresh.

"I don't know how to forgive you, Ryan," she said finally, her voice barely a whisper. "You hurt me so much, and now... now I have to think about this child. I don't know if I can move forward with you, but I can't carry this all alone either."

Ryan's voice softened. "I don't expect you to forgive me overnight. I don't expect you to just forget everything. But I'll be here. For you, and for our child. I'll do whatever it takes to prove that I care."

Hope didn't respond right away. The weight of her decision was heavy on her, and I could feel the struggle within her. She was caught between her own pain and the desire for a future that wasn't filled with regret.

I watched as Hope wiped a tear from her eye, looking out the window. "I don't know what to do," she said, her voice so small. "But I'll try. For the baby. For the future."

And in that moment, I knew we were all at the beginning of something new. The past wouldn't just disappear, but maybe—just maybe—we could start to rebuild. One piece at a time. For our daughter. For ourselves.

It wasn't going to be easy. Nothing about this was going to be easy. But it had to be done. For hope. For healing. For family.

XII

The Weight of Retribution

I couldn't have known then, but everything I had tried to protect Hope from, all the pain I'd shielded her from, would be overshadowed by something far worse. The past few weeks had been a blur of confusion and heartbreak, but nothing could have prepared me for the storm that was about to hit.

My father—he'd always been a man of principle, a protector of what he believed was right. When he found out about Ryan, what he had done to Hope, the betrayal, the pain... it triggered something inside him. I tried to warn him, tried to talk sense into him, but my father's anger was a force of nature, and once it was set in motion, there was no stopping it.

The night of the confrontation, I had no idea what was unfolding just a few miles away. Ryan was out with some friends, trying to drown the guilt of his past in whiskey and distractions. My father, in his fury, sought him out—his need for retribution overriding the faintest notion of mercy.

It ended in violence. My father's rage was too much for Ryan to handle, and before anyone could intervene, it was over. Ryan was dead.

I didn't know what to think when I heard the news. I didn't even process it at first. The world felt like it was falling apart in slow motion, pieces breaking away one by one. And then came the investigators, the questions, the accusations, the truth.

My father had killed Ryan. The investigation revealed everything—every detail, every step leading up to the murder. The weight of it all crushed me like an avalanche, leaving me gasping for air.

The man I had tried to shield, the man who had loved me despite everything... he had crossed a line. He had taken a life in the name of vengeance, and there was no turning back.

But it wasn't just the weight of my father's actions that shattered me. It was what came next. What followed the murder, what followed the wreckage of the lies, the pain, and the regret.

Hope.

Hope had been struggling for weeks now, wrestling with her emotions, the guilt of the secrets she had learned, the weight of everything that had been revealed to her. She had no more fight left. She couldn't see a way forward. In the midst of all the chaos, the heartbreak, and the family she no longer recognized, Hope made a decision that would haunt me forever.

She took poison.

I found her too late, slumped over, her delicate hands still clasping the note she had written. Her death was a silent scream in the night. She was gone—my daughter, my beautiful, fragile Hope—taken by her own hands.

The grief of her loss was unbearable, but the realization that her death had been in part caused by the mess we had made, the betrayal we had inflicted on her, felt like a cruel punishment.

The world spun, and the news hit like a tidal wave. Two deaths—Ryan's murder and Hope's tragic suicide—marked the end of something irreversible. The authorities worked tirelessly, the investigation unfolding in ways I couldn't have imagined. And as the evidence emerged, there was no escaping the truth.

Aisha . The same name that had been cursed, the same name that had sparked this spiral of destruction. I was arrested, charged with complicity for my father's actions. It didn't matter that I hadn't pulled the trigger, hadn't given him permission. It didn't matter that I had tried to stop him. The law saw the connections, the patterns of chaos we had all helped create, and I was held responsible.

The trial, the courtroom, the accusations—I couldn't escape them. The shame weighed heavily on my shoulders. I wanted to scream, to explain to the world that I didn't ask for any of this, that I never wanted this. I just wanted peace, a chance to heal the wounds I had inflicted on Hope, to fix the pieces of my broken past.

But nothing could bring Hope back. Nothing could undo my father's actions. And nothing could change the grief that had settled in my heart, the regret that lingered like a permanent stain.

Now, as I sit here, waiting for the verdict, the world feels hollow. My heart is heavy with the loss of both my daughter and the man I once loved. My father is behind bars, his actions condemning him as much as mine condemned me.

I tried so hard to fix things, to make everything right. But in the end, the pieces were shattered beyond repair.

And as the cold weight of my fate looms over me, I wonder—was it worth it? The lies, the secrets, the choices that led us here. Was it worth the destruction of everything I held dear?

I don't have an answer. And perhaps, I never will. But one thing I know for certain: the storm we created has left us all broken, and there is no coming back from it.

About Author

Prudance Vanessa Ndhlovu is a passionate storyteller who delves into themes of human relationships, resilience, and personal growth. Through her writing, she seeks to inspire and resonate with readers from all walks of life. Betrayed is a testament to her belief in the power of stories to heal and transform.

DISCUSSION QUESTIONS

1. How do Aisha's decisions shape the trajectory of her life, and could she have avoided some of the challenges she faced?
2. How does Samantha's influence push Aisha toward choices that conflict with her upbringing and values?
3. What role does Ryan play in both Aisha's downfall and her eventual redemption?
4. How does Aisha's relationship with her family evolve throughout the story?
5. What does the story suggest about the importance of parental guidance in navigating life's challenges?
6. How does the theme of faith manifest in Aisha's journey, and what role does it play in her moments of crisis?
7. What lessons does Aisha learn about love, trust, and forgiveness by the end of the story?
8. How does the relationship between Aisha and Hope explore the complexities of motherhood?
9. In what ways do societal pressures and judgment influence the decisions made by Aisha and her family?
10. How does the contrast between Samantha and Kate reflect the choices Aisha faces in her life?
11. How do Aisha's struggles with trust and betrayal shape her ability to form healthy relationships in the future?
12. What impact does Ryan's betrayal have on Aisha's sense of self-worth, and how does she rebuild her confidence?
13. How does Aisha's faith play a role in her ability to forgive herself and others?
14. In what ways does the story show that redemption is possible even after devastating mistakes?

15. What does Hope's journey reveal about the ripple effects of Aisha's choices on the next generation?

16. How does the revelation of Ryan's connection to Hope change the dynamics of all the characters involved?

17. How does the author use symbolism, such as Aisha's pink dress or the recurring theme of storms, to emphasize key moments in the story?

18. What role does resilience play in Aisha's journey, and how does she find strength to move forward despite the odds?

19. How does the tragic ending of the story impact your view of the characters and their choices?

20. What do you think the title Betrayed represents for each of the major characters in the story?

CONNECT WITH AUTHOR

I would love to hear your thoughts, reflections, and feedback on Betrayed. Feel free to connect with me through the following platforms:

WhatsApp: +918141191327

Email: nprudance9@gmail.com

LinkedIn: Prudance Ndhlovu

Your support and connection mean the world to me. Let's keep the conversation going!

Connect With Alphabet Club